BEST FRIENDS
UNDER THE SUN

Sharla Scannell Whalen

Illustrations by Virginia Kylberg

ABDO & Daughters
Minneapolis

Published by Abdo & Daughters, 4940 Viking Drive, Suite 622, Edina, Minnesota 55435.

Illustrations by Virginia Kylberg

Edited by Michele Blake and Ken Berg

Library of Congress Cataloging-in-Publication Data

Whalen, Sharla Scannell, 1960-
    Best Friends under the sun/Sharla Scannell Whalen;
illustrations by Virginia Kylberg.
        p.   cm. -- (Faithful friends)
        Summary: When a sculpture commemorating the pioneer spirit is finally unveiled, the subject matter amazes everyone in town, even the young visitor from England who has been dazzling the local girls.
        ISBN 1-56239-839-3
        [1. City and town life--Fiction. 2. Sculpture--Fiction.-]
I. Kylberg, Virginia, ill. II. Title. III. Series.
PZ7.W54558e   1997
[Fic]--dc21
                                                                                            97-38593
                                                                                                CIP
                                                                                                 AC

Table of Contents

CHAPTER ONE

STRAWBERRY FIELDS

Maggie Sullivan sat back on her heels and swiped a grimy hand across the untidy red curls on her brow. "Whew! The sun is really getting hot–and it's not even July yet." She reached for a strawberry in the basket, but her friend, Ellie Perry, swatted at her hand.

"Your mother warned us about you, Maggie," Ellie laughed.

Maggie groaned. "Mama can't forget about the time I came home with an empty bucket from a field full of strawberries. Boy, I had a stomachache that day!"

Maggie looked guiltily towards her little white house with slate-blue shutters, visible in the distance. An American flag hanging from the front porch appeared tiny from across the fields. The Sullivans lived on Hobson Street, at the eastern edge of Oakdale.

The Riordans, who farmed the fields opposite
Hobson Street, had invited Maggie and her friends
to help themselves to this year's abundant crop of
strawberries. There would be raspberries later on

and pumpkins in the fall.

"Do you know," began Hannah Olson, "this is the first time all four of us have been together since the wedding?"

"That's right," agreed Beth Dunstable, dropping two strawberries grown together into her container. "What a happy day that was!"

The four friends had been chosen to be flower girls for their teacher, Miss Delia Devine ... now Mrs. Henry Moore.

"My favorite moment was when the groom toasted the bride," remembered Beth. "He raised his glass of champagne and said that she was 'Devine.'"

"And she said, now that she had married him, she felt 'Moore Devine,'" Ellie added.

"That was so corny," moaned Maggie.

"I thought it was romantic," sighed Hannah.

"Well," said Ellie, "it was a great day. Ice cream and cake in all those pretty colors."

"To match our dresses," smiled Beth. It had been a "rainbow wedding"–everything in pink, peach, yellow, green, blue, and violet.

Today the girls all wore light summer frocks and straw hats. Beth's hat was trimmed with tiny

pink roses, Maggie's with daisies. Hannah and
Ellie had tied grosgrain ribbons around the crowns
of theirs, with matching bows swinging from the
ends of Hannah's braids.

Agreeing that they had gathered enough berries,
the foursome headed across the field, back to the
Sullivan house.

Three-year-old Daisy and six-year-old twins,
Aidan and Brigid, had come out to the front porch
to watch for the girls. All of the Sullivan children,
including Maggie's big brother, Kevin, had red
hair–each in a slightly different shade.

"May I have a strawberry?" asked Daisy
politely. She had very dainty manners. Hannah
held out her basket so that Daisy could choose one.
Hannah's little sister, Jennie, was just a year older
than Daisy.

"Hey," said Aidan, reaching into Beth's basket.
"Look at these Siamese strawberries, grown
together. Perhaps a spell was cast on them by a
magic sorcerer."

"A strawberry sorcerer?" giggled Brigid. "I
think they look like baskets of little red hearts."
She helped herself to a plump berry from her big
sister's basket. Brigid and Aidan were known for

their very vivid imaginations.

The younger children ran to play "sorcerer" as Maggie and her friends went around to the pump in the backyard to give the strawberries a rinse.

"It feels good to be together again," remarked Maggie. "I never thought I'd say this, but I miss school. At least we knew we'd see each other every day."

"Why don't we do some baking on Saturday?" suggested Hannah. The four girls had formed a baking company which they called "Best Bakers."

"Too hot," said Maggie. "We've been having cold suppers every night this week. Mama doesn't want to heat up the kitchen by cooking."

"Same at my house," piped Hannah.

"And mine," echoed Ellie. "So when are we going to get together again?"

"I want to see your bicycle when it arrives, Beth," said Maggie.

"A bicycle?" asked Hannah. "How exciting!"

"Papa ordered it from Newman's mail order catalog."

"Yes, we'll all have to meet at Beth's to see the bicycle," said Ellie. "But perhaps it won't arrive right away. So let's plan to get together soon."

"I imagine we'll have a party to welcome Edward," Beth said mysteriously. "We'll see each other then."

"Edward who?" demanded Maggie.

"Didn't I tell you?" asked Beth, her eyes twinkling. "My cousin Edward is coming to visit ... from England."

"From England?" exclaimed Hannah.

"Edward has finished school at Eton, and my uncle has rewarded him with a trip to America."

"So how old is he?"

"Nearly seventeen, I think," said Beth. "He's traveling with his valet. Papa says Barlow is quite a character. Barlow has worked for the Dunstable family since papa was a little boy."

"How long will they be staying?" asked Ellie.

"Several weeks," replied Beth, adjusting her hat.

"My word!" said Hannah, attempting an English accent.

"My mother doesn't like England very much," commented Maggie thoughtfully. "She says that some of the English treated the Irish very badly. For many years, it was against the law for Irish people to learn to read and write."

"That's how it was for slaves, too," noted Ellie.

The fact that her grandfather had fought in a black regiment in the Civil War to help end slavery made her feel good.

"That's disgraceful," burst out Beth. "What was the matter with those people?"

"They weren't *those* people," said Maggie. "They were *your* people. You're English. And those slave-owners were *our* people. We're white."

"Grandma says to remember that a lot of white people and black people fought and died to end a terrible system," Ellie said softly.

"Still, it makes me feel sad to think that there ever was such a thing," said Hannah.

"Me, too," said Beth. "I feel ashamed. And it's terrible that the English treated the Irish so badly, Maggie."

"I'm glad we live in America," said Maggie. "Maybe everyone will learn to live together here."

"That reminds me of the Lincoln Liberty contest. Grandma snipped the notice about it out of the paper for me," said Ellie.

"What's that?" asked Maggie.

"It's a writing contest for children, sponsored by the newspaper. *The Oakdale Observer* puts it on every year. The essay can be no longer than 500 words. The winner is announced on the Fourth of July."

"I'd have trouble writing 500 words. But I'll bet you could do it, Ellie," encouraged Beth. "Are you going to enter?"

"Well, the theme is 'The Road to Liberty.' Our conversation makes me think that one of the things people who walk the 'Road to Liberty' must learn to do is to get along. Our ancestors all came from different countries–mine from Africa, Maggie's from Ireland, Beth's from England, and Hannah's from Sweden. But because of our friendship, we all get along–despite our differences."

"I don't know," chuckled Maggie. "Last winter, I began to wonder." Beth and Maggie smiled at each other, remembering a quarrel they'd had in January.

"As my grandmother would say," concluded Ellie, "all's well that ends well."

"And as cousin Edward might say," giggled Beth, "right-o!"

CHAPTER TWO

EDWARD THE CONQUEROR

The night before Edward's arrival, Beth and her father had examined the big globe in his oak-paneled library, tracing the route of Edward's journey.

Looking at the map of England, Mr. Dunstable told Beth about his childhood there. He had been born in America, but his father had wanted him in the same English schools which the Dunstables had always attended.

Beth's great-grandfather, Henry George Dunstable, had been the first to come to America. "He was a second son, you see," explained her father. "In English families, the first son inherits the family home and property. Great-grandpa Dunstable thought he would find more opportunities in America. But he sent my father to school in England. And my father sent me."

"And you met Mama in London," Beth said softly. Beth's parents lived apart, and it still sometimes made her sad.

"That's right," Mr. Dunstable nodded. "She belongs in a big cosmopolitan city. It was a mistake to think she could be happy out here. She loves living in Paris, now. And she'll be visiting here again before long," he said, looking closely at Beth.

"Your mother came from Surrey. Barlow is from Surrey, too. He always said that Kent can't hold a candle to it. Now let's find Kent ... here it is. That's where Edward will have begun his journey."

About two weeks earlier, Edward had left the Dunstable ancestral home in Kent, just south of London. He'd traveled to Southampton by train and joined the ship there for the ocean crossing. In New York City, Edward boarded another train, taking him across New Jersey, Pennsylvania, Ohio, Indiana, and finally, Illinois. He transferred in Chicago for the ride west to Oakdale.

They'd had such a good time looking at the globe, Beth hadn't wanted to bring up a subject which had lately been very much on her mind.

She'd already discussed it with her father, but she was hoping he would change his opinion. "I'll talk to him tomorrow," she had decided.

This morning, Beth waited for an opportunity to speak with her father in private. She didn't think her Aunt Mary, who lived with them, would be a sympathetic listener. But there was no chance before they set out for the train station. Mr. Dunstable was detained in his study by a fellow member of the Town Council until the last minute. In the hustle of the carriage ride, Beth had only time to begin, "Father, about this statue the Council has commissioned ..."

Mr. Dunstable cut her off. "We've been over that twice already, Beth! Here we are at the station."

They arrived on the platform just a few minutes before the train roared down the tracks from Chicago and points east, its whistle blaring ahead across the Illinois prairie.

"I'll bet he's going to be exhausted, Papa," remarked Beth. "And it's such a hot day." She looked up at the deep blue sky, overlaid with a shimmering haze.

"Oh, I don't know," said Mr. Dunstable.

"Edward was tireless as a child. Now he's past sixteen, he probably has more energy than ever."

The train came puffing in, "Chicago and Western" emblazoned on its tender. The engine let off steam as it came to a stop in front of the little station. With the hissing steam, clanking coupling rods, and clanging bell, it made a tremendous noise.

Beth put her hands up under the brim of her straw hat to cover her ears. The hat was tied with pale green and chocolate-colored ribbons, to complement her dress.

A milling crowd seemed to appear on the platform from nowhere, waiting to meet passengers already descending the metal steps from the coaches.

Beth and her father scanned those emerging from the first class car. Suddenly, there was a commotion as a tall young man in a very fine summer suit hesitated in the doorway. Behind him, a voice was calling from the train car, "Eddy! Eddy, wait! You've forgotten your bat!"

"That must be Edward," Beth declared to her father. "How handsome he is."

"Ah," Mr. Dunstable muttered, as a young girl

passed forward a long wooden object. "It's not a bat at all. It's a croquet mallet."

"Oh, Eddy," yet another young girl was calling from the window of the train. "Write to me! You will write to me?"

Cousin Edward looked back. "Don't worry, old girl!"

Beth and her father exchanged glances. "Something tells me this visit is going to be most diverting," Mr. Dunstable said in an undertone. He then stepped forward with his hand outstretched. "Welcome to America, Edward! It looks as though you've already made some friends."

"It's grand to see you, Uncle Charles. And yes, we had a jolly time on the journey from Chicago," grinned Edward.

"He certainly gets acquainted quickly," Beth thought to herself.

Edward's brown hair was thick and wavy; his eyes were bright and blue. He had an English complexion: very fair skin and ruddy cheeks. His light tan jacket looked as freshly pressed as though he had just put it on. And his high paper collar was crisp. He carried a light brown bowler hat under one arm. A thin mustache was struggling to establish itself above his upper lip.

"You've met my daughter Beth," said Mr. Dunstable. "But it was so many years ago, I imagine neither one of you can recall."

"You look like a pistachio ice-cream cone in that dress and hat, Beth. And of course I remember you," smiled Edward expansively. "How could I forget such lovely blonde hair?"

Mr. Dunstable cleared his throat. "Actually, she was bald as a billiard ball, the last time you saw her. Beth was just six months old when her mother and I took her to England to visit her grandparents."

"'Twas nary a hair on her head," said a voice from behind Mr. Dunstable's shoulder.

"Barlow!" exclaimed Beth's father affectionately, turning around to shake hands with a slight man with graying hair. "And just like you to sneak up on one. How fine it is to see you."

"Very good of you, sir," Barlow bowed. "It's been nearly 10 years since we've had the pleasure of seeing you at Duns Manor."

"We all have a great deal to catch up on," said Mr. Dunstable. "I'm such an American these days, I've given up most English customs. But in honor of your visit, we'll all have tea!"

CHAPTER THREE

BICYCLE BLUNDER

Beth was waiting for her father in the carriage house. She was expecting Ellie, Maggie, and Hannah, too. Her bicycle had arrived early that morning, and she had just finished removing the various pieces from the packing box.

The Dunstable carriage house stood out behind the home under the shade of a towering elm tree. It was one of Beth's favorite spots, especially on a hot day. The carriage house was always quiet, dark, and cool.

It was hotter up under the rafters, where the toboggan the girls had used last winter was stored. Beth glanced up at it and rubbed her forehead. She'd gotten quite a knock in a sled accident caused by the reckless Murgatroyd Forsythe.

"He's a rat," Beth said aloud, recalling their most recent quarrel.

"I know who you mean!" chuckled Ellie,

peeking around the corner of the wide carriage house doors. Hannah and Maggie popped out, too.

"You're remembering that bump on the head you got because of Murg," suggested Maggie.

"Well yes ... and no," answered Beth. "I did think of that. But I'm more annoyed about what he said on Founder's Day."

"You mean about the statue the Town Council is having made for Central Park?" asked Hannah. "He said it's going to be based on his great-grandfather?"

"That's what he thinks!" Beth frowned.

"Pretty self-centered of him. But that's Murg for you. Whom do you think the statue should portray?" asked Maggie.

"Why, *my* great-grandfather, of course!" Beth exclaimed.

Ellie chuckled. "That's Beth for you! You're as bad as he is."

"No, I'm not!" Beth protested. "What did Murg's great-grandfather ever do for this town? Why, Henry George Dunstable ..."

Just then, Beth's father entered, and she broke off the conversation. Mr. Dunstable did not agree with Beth's opinion. He'd said that the stonemason had been told to create a statue depicting "Pioneer Spirit." He agreed with the Town Council's final decision–the statue wasn't meant to look like any particular founding member of the town. It was to represent the scores of pioneers who had pushed west from the original 13 colonies.

Sixty years earlier, in the 1830s, the Midwest was the frontier. Pioneers from Pennsylvania stopped here along the DuPage River and put roots down into the Illinois prairie. Their lives were full of long, hard work–out of which came a beautiful town. These were the people the statue was meant to honor.

"Where is that new bicycle? Let's have a look, Beth," said Mr. Dunstable now.

"Here it is, father. I've pulled the pieces out of the box, but there doesn't seem to be any printed instructions."

"Hmm," said Mr. Dunstable, scratching his head, thereby disarraying his neatly combed brown hair. "What's to be done?"

"Father," giggled Beth, "don't let Edward find you with your hair looking mussed. He won't want to be seen with you."

"That boy does spend a great deal of time on his grooming," agreed Mr. Dunstable. "Agnes said Barlow took hot water up to his room twice this morning." Agnes was the Dunstable's housekeeper, and she didn't take kindly to strange valets in her kitchen.

"What is Edward like?" asked Maggie curiously.

"He's very handsome," answered Beth.

"He's a dandy," added Mr. Dunstable.

"He told me I looked like a peppermint ice cream cone this morning," laughed Beth, looking down at her pink and white striped dress. "And do you know he's already made two 'conquests'? He met two girls on the train–he had one of them carrying his croquet mallet, the other was pleading that he write to her."

Just as Mr. Dunstable had taken an inventory of the bicycle components lying on the carriage house floor, a messenger from the courthouse appeared. The Town Council members were being summoned for a special meeting with the mayor.

"Sorry, Miss Pink," said Mr. Dunstable, using his affectionate nickname for Beth, who had a weakness for that color. "Business before pleasure." As he rose and dusted off his hands, he saw Edward approaching and added, "Perhaps this gentleman will help you with your bicycle."

"With pleasure," said Edward, smiling at the girls. "But I warn you, I'm not very good with mechanical things."

Beth introduced her friends, who greeted Edward shyly.

Edward removed his tan jacket, revealing a creamy white shirt, very neatly pressed, and a light brown vest. With a dazzling smile, he asked Maggie to hold the jacket. She accepted with a grimace, although folding it carefully over her arm.

"Now then," he said, as he attacked the pile of parts. His movements seemed decisive, as he attached one piece to another.

"Finished!" Edward proclaimed in what seemed like a very short time. He stepped back to survey his work.

"I think the steering wheel is on backwards," announced Maggie.

"Never!" said Edward.

"And the pedals don't look right," said Hannah softly.

"Don't you think so?" Edward returned.

"And I don't think the wheels will turn in that position," worried Beth.

"Oh dear," said Edward.

"Is that piece A attached to piece C?" asked
Ellie, studying the instructions she had rescued
from beneath the leftover parts.

"I don't know. I removed all the lettered
labels on the pieces," answered Edward. "In short,
I'm afraid I've muffed it."

"What do we do now?" moaned Beth.

"Don't worry, we can take it to Mr. Lockhart, the blacksmith," said Maggie. She handed Edward his jacket.

"Bully for you!" said Edward with an embarrassed grin.

"Is he calling me a bully?" Maggie asked.

"No," said Beth. "He's saying, 'good for you.' He likes your suggestion."

"I like it, too," said Hannah. "I've heard that Mr. Lockhart is working on a design for a flying machine. I would love to see it!" Hannah was fond of all aspects of math and science.

As Edward and the girls loaded the tortured-looking bicycle onto the wagon, Beth dashed into her father's study. She silently removed a miniature painting in an oval frame from the wall, and slipped it into the pocket of her "peppermint" dress.

CHAPTER FOUR

LIBBY LOCKHART

Mr. Lockhart was the town inventor as well as blacksmith. Hannah was excited to be visiting his workshop. Beth was also pleased, but for a very different reason. She knew that Mr. Carroll, the stonemason, was working on the statue for Central Park at Mr. Lockhart's shop.

Ellie and Maggie sat up on the wagon seat with Edward, while Hannah and Beth rode in the wagon box with the bicycle. Beth patted it, "Poor thing."

As they drove through town, two high school girls in front of McGuire's Books and Notions called out, "Hi, Eddy!"

"Cheerio!" Edward called back.

"Those must be conquests numbers three and four," Beth whispered to Hannah.

"How in the world do you know those young ladies?" Ellie asked.

Before Edward could answer, another female

voice cried out, "Eddy, Eddy! Don't forget you promised to call!"

"Morning, old girl," Edward tossed back to another young lady, who giggled as though he had said something clever.

"It's as though he's lived here all his life," said Maggie.

"That was number five," Hannah whispered to Beth.

"Edward, how do you know these girls?" demanded Ellie.

"Why, I took a little stroll around yesterday afternoon after I arrived. Wanted to get acquainted with the town a bit."

"Acquainted with the girls of the town, you mean," accused Maggie under her breath.

"The same thing happened on the train from Chicago," Beth told Hannah. "They flock to him like bees to honey."

"I wonder why," Hannah whispered to Beth. "He looks like an advertisement for fine men's clothing that's walked out of the newspaper. He doesn't seem quite real."

"Papa says he thinks the girls fall for Edward's British accent," confided Beth.

They drove out to the end of Eagle Street where the blacksmith's shop stood. The trade suited Mr. Lockhart, since tinkering and building things were what he liked to do best. When he wasn't smithing, he was working on designs for all sorts of inventions.

Hannah was in luck today. Not only was Mr. Lockhart working on his drawings for a flying machine, his daughter Libby was seated at a table working on a model of it. It looked like an elaborate kite.

Beth was in luck, too. Mr. Carroll was busy at carving the statue. His friend Mr. Lockhart had offered his large, open workshop for the huge stone that he was now chiseling. Since Mr. Carroll spent many of his afternoons there in any case, this suited them both.

Mr. Carroll looked up to greet the group with the twisted bicycle. Mr. Lockhart already had wrenches out and said it wouldn't take but a minute to repair.

Hannah and Maggie stepped over to see the model of the flying machine. Edward joined them (Libby being a very pretty girl with snapping hazel eyes and honey-brown hair.) "I suppose that will be conquest number six for Edward," Beth whispered to Ellie.

"I wouldn't be too sure," Ellie whispered back.

"I've met Libby before. She's not like those silly high school girls."

Beth and Ellie asked Mr. Carroll how the pioneer statue was coming along. The lower part still looked like a formless lump, but a human torso was emerging from the upper portion.

"Oh, good," said Beth. "You haven't begun on the face yet."

"No," said Mr. Carroll. "I usually do that last. But this time, I may end up doing the legs and feet last–because I can't decide what to show our spirited pioneer doing. Should he be standing with his trusty dog, holding a rifle–setting out to hunt for his family's supper? Or perhaps he's a farming pioneer, with a handplow by his side. Then again, maybe he should be a rancher. What do you girls think?"

"Well actually, Mr. Carroll, I do have an idea for you," said Beth, drawing the miniature from her pocket. "Perhaps you've heard of Henry Dunstable, one of the founders of Oakdale. He was responsible for laying out many of the streets, and ... I was thinking that perhaps his likeness could provide some inspiration. He had a very fine face."

"Yes, he did," said Mr. Carroll, studying the tiny painting. "But this leaves me in a rather difficult situation. You see, just this morning, I had a similar suggestion–but on behalf of a different founding father of the town. The young man insisted on leaving the portrait of his great-grandfather. Here it is."

"Don't tell me," Beth groaned.

"It was Murg, wasn't it?" Ellie asked.

"That's right, young Master Forsythe."

"He beat you to it, Beth," laughed Ellie.

Mr. Carroll leaned against his piece of stone, studying the two portraits. "A pretty pickle," he said. "Master Forsythe mentioned that his uncle is on the Town Council. I understand your father is also on the Council, Miss Dunstable?"

"Yes, sir," said Beth, reaching for the likeness of her great-grandfather. "But he would be quite annoyed if he knew I had brought this to show you. He said the Council had given you the freedom to create your own idea of the 'Pioneer Spirit.'"

"Yes, that's true. But it's a bit awkward, having two members on the Council descended from competing pioneers." Mr. Carroll frowned at his piece of stone.

"Ellie!" called Hannah from the other side of the workroom. "I was telling Libby about your ideas for the Lincoln Essay. She is very interested in Rights for Women."

As she crossed the room with Ellie, Beth glanced at her cousin. Edward's face bore a sour expression, as though he had failed to charm Libby. Perhaps he was annoyed that Libby was more interested in Rights for Women than she was in him.

"Are the rest of you girls entering the writing contest, too?" asked Libby.

"No," answered Hannah. "Ellie is our budding writer ... and reader, too. She's just like your brother Aidan, Maggie. She never goes anywhere without a little book hidden in her pocket. What is it today, Ellie?"

Ellie pulled out a little copy of *The Little Princess*.

"I'd love to hear about your essay, Ellie," said Libby. "What is the topic?"

"The Road to Liberty," responded Ellie. "I was thinking that the road to liberty can mean different things to different people. It was the love of liberty that brought many people to America–the Pilgrims and other religious groups, for instance. And it was on that same road that a war was fought for freedom from England. No offense intended, Edward," Ellie said, smiling at him.

"Right you are," he said, glancing at Libby.

"And since the name of the contest is the Lincoln Essay," Ellie went on, "I thought the Civil War was particularly appropriate, too. That was another step on the road to liberty, this time for black Americans.

"I was also thinking about the road to liberty that we are still walking. Women have been organizing to fight for their rights for quite some time now."

Beth noticed that Mr. Carroll was now staring at them and eavesdropping on the conversation.

"What a wonderful idea for an essay!" cried Libby.

"But who would take it seriously?" questioned Edward.

Libby frowned at him. "Many women–and men, too–would take it very seriously, indeed. And it's a 'Road to Liberty' that women have been walking for a very long time. I wonder how much longer we'll have to walk it before we get even the right to vote."

"Miss Devine ... or rather, Mrs. Moore ... talked about that very thing last year," said Ellie.

"Oh, do you know Mrs. Moore?" asked Libby eagerly. "I read in the newspaper that she was the first woman in the county who was able to keep her job after she was married."

"She was our teacher last year," said Maggie.

"I would love to meet her someday," said Libby. "She's the most outspoken woman in the town about women's rights."

"Libby," exclaimed Beth, "you must come to the lawn party my father is giving at our house on Saturday afternoon. Mrs. Moore will be there and I know she would love to meet you. And it will give you and Ellie a chance to continue your conversation."

"I'd love to come, Beth. It will be lovely to meet Mrs. Moore. Is the reception being given for the newlyweds?"

"Actually, my father is hosting it as a welcoming party for Edward," said Beth.

Libby shot a dark glance at Edward, looking as though she wished she hadn't accepted so quickly an invitation to a party in his honor.

"Come on, Edward," said Maggie. "Let's see how many conquests you can make on the way home."

Chapter Five

Lawn Party for Edward

"Good morning, all," said Edward, coming into the dining room bright and early on Saturday. "Beth," he said, surveying her with approval, "you look like tutti-frutti this morning."

"Thank you, Edward," said Beth, looking down at her pink dress with rose-colored sash.

"I hadn't realized that tutti-frutti had come to England," remarked Aunt Mary dryly.

"Oh, it hasn't. But I sampled some at Brown's Ice Cream Depot with Miss Evelyn Beebe the other afternoon."

"You're quite the man about town, Edward," said Mr. Dunstable.

"Thank goodness for the sun this morning," said Edward, changing the subject. "After two days of rain, I was beginning to feel as though I were back in England!"

"I'm sure you're relieved we don't have to

cancel the lawn party this afternoon," said Beth. "You must be eager to wear that linen suit of yours."

Edward looked at Beth suspiciously. He was just beginning to understand the teasing remarks of his American cousin and her friends.

Beth's home stood on the shady corner of Jefferson and Elm in Oakdale's fashionable central district. Jefferson was a lovely, wide street with flower beds down the middle. The Dunstable house was freshly painted light pink with gingerbread trim in white and grey. The gingerbread ran atop two little porches on either side of the house and across the large veranda in front.

The house and lawn were festive today, with a white marquee set up to protect the refreshments table from unexpected rain showers. (And to guard it against an unexpected canine guest, Beth's little white dog, Snowflake, had been shut safely into her pink bedroom.) A long table held Staffordshire platters of sugar cookies cut in the shape of stars, several layer cakes, and a tray of the Best Baker's muffins.

For the lawn party, they had invented "Strawberry Shortcake Muffins." These were baked with a mixture of finely chopped strawberries and sweetened cream. Each was topped with a sliced strawberry, looking like a little heart.

Beth was excited because she had convinced Agnes to serve the new flavored gelatins which were featured in the front window of the grocer's store. There was an array of all four flavors: strawberry, lemon, orange, and raspberry. Beth looked at Edward curiously when he called them "jellies."

"It's called Jell-O here," said Beth good-naturedly. "Jelly is like jam."

Each day, Edward and Beth seemed to find some new difference between their respective versions of English.

Beth's friends were the first to arrive. Mr. Dunstable had invited his fellow members of the Town Council and the school board to bring their families–many of whom had daughters. Edward was already enjoying the company of two talkative belles. But he kept inspecting the gathering crowd.

"Looking for someone, Edward?" Maggie stepped up to ask him.

"No," said Edward. "Just admiring the decorations."

But after Libby arrived, Edward's eyes never left her. Soon he excused himself from a little group of attentive females and approached Libby, who was talking to Ellie and her friends.

"I was thinking about Ellie's essay," Edward said. "She has some good ideas, but surely she is wrong in thinking that the Rights for Women movement has been around for a long time. Certainly it's just a newfangled fad and won't last long."

"The movement is over a hundred years old," Libby informed Edward. She turned away from him and spoke to Ellie. "I brought you a book about the history of the women's suffrage movement by Harriet Jane Robinson. I thought it might help with your essay. It says that way back in 1774, Abigail Adams wrote to her husband–he later became President Adams–while he was in Philadelphia attending the First Continental Congress."

"The men there were working on a new structure of government. Abigail told her husband to 'remember the ladies' when they wrote about the rights of the states. Let me read it to you: Mrs. Adams said, 'Do not put such unlimited power in the hands of the husbands. If particular care and attention is not paid to the ladies, we are determined to foment a rebellion, and will not hold ourselves bound by any laws in which we have no voice or representation.' "

"Of course, two years later, the Second

Continental Congress came up with the Declaration of Independence, which specified that all men are created equal," said Mr. Lockhart, joining them.

"I wonder what Abigail Adams had to say to the mister when he came home with a copy of that!" said Maggie.

"Here's exactly what she said," continued Libby, picking up the book. " 'I cannot say that I think you are very generous to the ladies, for, while you are proclaiming peace and good will to all men, emancipating all nations, you insist upon retaining absolute power over wives. But you must remember, that absolute power, like most other things which are very bad, is most likely to be broken.' "

"I wish I could have been a mouse under the table for some of the Adams' dinner table conversations," commented Beth.

"Abigail Adams put the whole Women's Rights Movement into a nutshell," said Ellie thoughtfully.

"I must admit, I had no idea that it was such an established movement," said Edward. "But come, ladies, croquet has begun." Edward was already carrying the mallet he had brought from England.

Evelyn Beebe was selecting a mallet from a rack standing on the lawn. "I haven't the foggiest idea

how to play this game," she said, gazing at Edward meaningfully.

"Allow me to show you," he said. "And I can tell you about the ancient history of the game. It's well over a hundred years old, though I don't believe Abigail Adams played it," he said, with a glance over his shoulder at Libby.

Libby pretended not to hear.

"Actually," said Edward, "croquet was invented by men in thirteenth century France. The wickets were hoops made of willow branches."

"Ellie," said Libby loudly, selecting a mallet of her own, "Did you know that there have been Women's Rights conferences for nearly fifty years?" She gave the wooden ball a hard whack, darting a glance at Edward.

"Of course, in its modern form," said Edward, "croquet has only been played for the last sixty years or so." He hit his ball with a loud crack and gazed defiantly at Libby.

CHAPTER SIX

FLYING MACHINE

Libby had invited the four friends to a launching of her model of the flying machine that her father had designed. Beth told Edward she was sure Libby wouldn't mind if he came, too–but he declined.

"I think it's driving him crazy that he's finally met a girl who doesn't think he's the cat's meow," Beth told her father in private.

On the day of the launch, Hannah, Beth, and Maggie met Ellie at her grandmother's quaint red house, west of town. They joined the Lockharts on a rocky ridge out near the quarry. Mr. Carroll and several other friends of Mr. Lockhart had also come to observe. Some boys from school had shown up, too–including Ben Tarken and Daniel O'Leary.

Hannah's father had been clipping articles about flying machines from the newspaper for her.

She had also borrowed a book called *Progress in Flying Machines* from the library. And she was delighted to learn that Libby and Mr. Lockhart knew the author, the famous civil engineer, Octave Chanute. In fact, not long before, the Lockharts had gone out to the Indiana dunes to witness the flights of several gliders.

"I hope you won't mind, Mr. Lockhart," said Hannah. "I've invited my brothers to join us. They like flying machines, too. In fact, I see them coming now."

"Oh, Rachel is with them!" whooped Beth. "And she's bringing her baby. Hooray!"

"The more the merrier," smiled Mr. Lockhart. "I just hope the flight of this little glider is worth watching. I have some concerns about the design."

Hannah introduced her older sister, Rachel, and brothers, Joshua, Aaron, and Jason, to the Lockharts.

Beth asked to hold Baby Mae. The little one's full name was Naomi Mae, but everyone seemed to feel that the nickname suited her better.

"Will you be using Pratt trussing, sir?" Joshua asked Mr. Lockhart.

"That's right," said Mr. Lockhart, sounding

impressed. "You Olsons know your flying machines!"

"We're interested in your work on the pioneer monument, too, Mr. Carroll," said Aaron.

"When will it be unveiled?" asked Rachel, retrieving Baby Mae from Beth, who had become entangled in the child's long white dress and pink blanket.

"At a ceremony on the Fourth of July," Mr. Carroll responded, holding out his index finger for the baby to grasp.

"Of course," said Rachel. "The children's choir will be singing at the courthouse for the festivities. Hannah has been practicing for her solo with her voice teacher, Mrs. McGuire."

"What will you be singing?" Libby inquired.

"The choir will sing 'The Battle Hymn of the Republic.' And my solo is the verse beginning, 'He has sounded forth the trumpet that shall never call retreat.' Polly Sanders, from our class at school, has a solo, too."

Joshua turned the subject back to the one at hand. "I've read about the Katydid," he remarked to Mr. Lockhart.

"A beautiful craft," Libby's father replied. "But

too many wings! I've patterned my own flying machine on the Chanute/Herring Biplane. You really must join us on the dunes this autumn. A number of aviators will be bringing their creations. And now for mine ... and Libby's. Come on Hannah, you can help."

Mr. Lockhart carried the model to a hill on the far side of the quarry. He licked a finger and held it up to determine direction of the wind. Atop the slope, he handed the model to Hannah. It was attached to a thin cord, which Mr. Lockhart unwound as he backed down the hillside. Hannah positioned the flying machine above her head and ran about ten feet with it, then thrust it out over the quarry. Mr. Lockhart cut the string when certain it had launched successfully, allowing the model to soar to a respectable altitude.

"It's going to crash," said Beth anxiously.

"You might be surprised," Joshua predicted.

And they were. The model flew out high above the quarry, caught a lucky air current and soared a little higher. It crossed the wide quarry and set out for Quarry Road before they all stopped staring dumbfounded and began to run after it. They could see it starting to dip, then disappear behind a line of

trees along the road.

Emerging onto Quarry Road, the group drew to a stop. The boys began to laugh. There was Grandma Perry's house sitting primly inside its white fence. And there in her oak tree perched the model of the flying machine. Mrs. Perry had slumped into a chair on her porch, looking as though lightning had struck before her eyes. Ellie's calico cat, Cleo, jumped into Mrs. Perry's lap with one big, scared bounce.

"Grandma!" called Ellie. "Are you all right?"

"I'm fine, but wait until you see the great big bird perched in my oak tree." Her eyes were twinkling now. "I won't deny that it gave me–and Cleo–quite a turn. I knew you were all planning to launch a flying machine today, but I didn't think it would land on my head!"

CHAPTER SEVEN

NORTH SHORE ADVENTURE

Despite the surprise landing in Grandma Perry's oak tree, the test of the little glider was considered a great success. Mr. Lockhart was planning to build a full-scale flying machine, now that he knew his design was sky-worthy.

After the launch, Mrs. Moore and Libby pursued the discussion they had begun at the Dunstable lawn party. Ellie participated, too–though the rest of the girls had to admit they were getting a tad tired of talking about Rights for Women.

"They're not too interested just now," Mrs. Moore whispered to Libby. "But their time will come."

One thing the girls had not tired of was analyzing Edward's attitude towards Libby.

"She's brought Edward the Conqueror to his knees," Hannah had giggled.

The four were pleased to be included with Libby in an invitation Mrs. Moore extended on behalf of her aunt, Mrs. Martin-Mitchell. She had often bought muffins from them when they rang the front bell at her home. And since then, Hannah, Beth, Maggie, and Ellie had been frequent guests at Pine Craig.

Now they were to visit Mrs. Martin-Mitchell's summer cottage on the North Shore of Lake Michigan. They would take the train with Mrs. Moore. Aunt Mary was invited as chaperone, too. And Mrs. Martin-Mitchell's carriage would meet them for the last leg of the trip.

Edward was included as well.

"I wonder if he'll get any farther with Libby," Beth whispered.

He certainly didn't make any progress on the train. Edward sat as far from Libby as possible. He chatted with another traveler, a young woman riding from Aurora to Calumet. Libby looked out the window or talked to Mrs. Moore.

"What do you have in that satchel, Ellie? I hope it's something to eat." Maggie smacked her lips hungrily.

"Sorry, Maggie," chuckled Ellie. "It's just a bag of books. I've brought *Eight Cousins, The Five Little Peppers and How They Grew*, and *Countess Kate*."

"Why so many?" inquired Beth. "You'll never have time to read them all."

"It feels good to know that I have a book along for every mood," smiled Ellie, patting her reading material. "They make me feel sort of 'safe.' "

"You're going to be a librarian when you grow up," predicted Hannah.

"Or a writer," Maggie put in.

All of the girls were wearing sailor suits and flat "boater" hats today. Beth's was yellow with red trim—and for once, Beth thought Edward would fail to find a flavor of ice cream with which to compare her. But he had surprised her. "Vanilla ... with raspberry sauce," he had quipped while assisting her onto the train. Beth burst out laughing.

Everyone was hot, dusty, and thirsty when they reached Mrs. Martin-Mitchell's charming cottage. It was smaller than many of the grand homes on the lake, but it was still bigger than most in Oakdale.

"Somehow, 'cottage' doesn't seem like the right name for this place," said Maggie.

"It's beautiful," said Libby. "Thank you so much for inviting me, Mrs. Martin-Mitchell."

Mrs. Martin-Mitchell welcomed them all and led the way to a long picnic table set out by the lake. It was covered with a yellow cloth and held a sumptuous lunch.

"Does that sailboat belong to you?" Maggie asked Mrs. Moore's aunt, helping herself to fried chicken and deviled eggs.

"Yes," said Mrs. Martin-Mitchell. "Perhaps you'd like to take it out this afternoon? Do we have any sailors among us?"

"Yes, ma'am," bowed Edward. "I've been sailing a number of times. I was also on the rowing team at Eaton, and I hope to row for Oxford next year."

"Show-off," mumbled Libby under her breath.

Edward turned to her. "Do you sail, Libby?"

"No," she said. "But I must admit I've always wanted to learn. I'm interested in it from a scientific point of view."

"Of course," said Edward. "Scientific."

Libby and Mrs. Moore began to discuss politics. After a time, Edward commented, "This Rights for Women is certainly a busy little movement, isn't it? But I'd never heard of it until I came here."

"The movement is even more active in England, I believe, than it is here. Is it possible you've really never heard of it, Edward?" wondered Libby.

"I suppose I may have, but no lady of my

acquaintance would ever dignify it with her interest," Edward returned.

"We have no lords and ladies here," Libby sounded disdainful, but she looked stung. "America is a democracy."

"We may have no lords here," announced Aunt Mary unexpectedly, "but we do have ladies. You are presently in the company of a number of them, Edward. And in America, I like to think we have gentlemen."

Edward looked abashed. "I'm sorry I spoke impolitely," he apologized.

That afternoon, the four friends, Edward, and Libby took the sailboat out onto the choppy waters of the Great Lake.

While Libby was busy examining the rigging, Edward warned the girls to duck whenever he told them to do so.

They hadn't gone far when he declared the water too rough for a good sail with so many novices. He began to turn the craft back to the shore.

"Duck!" he shouted as the boom came around. Hannah, Ellie, Maggie, and Beth all crouched down, but Libby wasn't quite quick enough.

"Bang!" It hit her square across the back and

knocked her into the lake with a great splash.

Edward took off his jacket and dove right in after her. The two of them came up coughing, his arms around Libby tightly.

Edward urged Hannah, Ellie, and Maggie to sit on the opposite side of the boat so it wouldn't tip over as he hoisted Libby back up, assisted by Beth.

Safely back on board, she sat on the deck, her sailor suit dripping. "I guess I forgot to mention I can't swim," she said with a weak grin.

"Look on this as your first lesson," said Edward gallantly. "First I insult you, then I knock you in the water."

"I'm surprised you're not furious. I hope your dress isn't ruined."

"My clothes are not my main concern. My dress will dry in the sun in no time."

Edward turned the boat toward shore. They were all relieved to reach the safety of dry land.

"Look," pointed Beth, seeing Mrs. Moore approaching with a tray. "Ice cream."

"Umm," said Maggie. "Three flavors."

"I adore ice cream," said Libby.

"Do you?" asked Edward. "And would you believe," he said teasingly. "Ice cream is older than Rights for Women."

"Not more history!" complained Maggie.

"If it's about ice cream, I won't mind," said Beth, selecting a dish of maple nut from the tray.

"Once upon a time," began Edward, "King Charles I of England put on a state dinner. After many delicacies had been served, the guests declared it the finest meal they had ever been served.

But the best was yet to come. The King's chef had prepared a marvelous surprise, unlike any dessert seen before. Served in crystal bowls, it looked like snow, yet was creamy, sweet, and smooth.

Charles was delighted with the success of the invention. But he wanted the secret of the recipe for this frozen confection reserved for the King's table, and he paid the chef hundreds of pounds a year to keep silent."

"What a wonderful story!" sighed Hannah, savoring her dish of chocolate ice cream.

"But did the chef keep the secret?" Maggie wanted to know.

"Yes," said Edward. "At least until 1649."

"What happened then?" asked Ellie.

"Poor King Charles lost his head," said Edward sadly.

"Edward!" protested Beth. "You've ruined a perfectly good story."

"It's the truth," he shrugged.

Libby laughed.

"But when did ice cream come to America?" wondered Ellie.

"Very early," said Libby. "We had Abigail Adams

to thank for the beginning of Rights for Women. And we have another president's wife to thank for popularizing ice cream in this country. Dolly Madison arranged for it to be served at the Inaugural Ball given for her husband, James. Presidents' wives have been quite influential, you see."

"Very," agreed Edward with a smile. But his face took on a more solemn expression. "Tell us more about that first Rights for Women convention," he said.

Libby looked surprised, but she complied. She began to tell him about the revision of the Declaration of the Independence which the women at the convention had devised.

The four friends had had enough of such serious dialogue, and chose this moment to gather up the empty dishes and spoons. As they returned to the cottage, Beth glanced back over her shoulder. Edward was concentrating on Libby more seriously. "The 1848 Declaration of Sentiments and Resolutions outlined the main issues and goals for the women's movement ..." she was saying. And he was listening.

CHAPTER EIGHT

THE GLORIOUS FOURTH

"Did you hear?" Beth called to Maggie from her front porch. "Ellie has won the Lincoln Liberty Contest!"

Maggie ran the rest of the way up Jefferson Street to Beth's house. The four girls had agreed to meet there before heading to the courthouse for the Fourth of July celebration.

Beth handed the morning paper to Maggie. "Look! It's right here on the front page."

"This is wonderful!" breathed Maggie, scanning the essay.

"And here comes the winner herself!" proclaimed Edward as Ellie and Hannah came around the corner from Elm Street.

Hannah carried a copy of the newspaper under one arm. "Have you heard the news?" she sang out joyfully.

"What do we say first?" asked Beth. "Happy Birthday or Congratulations??"

"Or Happy Fourth of July?" suggested Maggie.

Ellie smiled. "Don't forget you're all coming out to our house for cake this afternoon. Grandma is so proud about the essay. She says that winning the contest is my birthday present to myself."

"I should say so!" agreed Edward.

"I'm afraid we're going to have to hurry over to Central Park," said Hannah. "The choir director told us to be early."

Edward accompanied the foursome to the courthouse. The girls were dressed in shades of red, white, and blue. Beth wore red with white trimming. "A cherry sundae," Edward said as he walked beside her, "with whipped cream on top." They all laughed.

Approaching the courthouse, they saw tables set out, with refreshments for sale. "Say," said Maggie, "that gives me an idea. We should sell muffins here next year."

"That would be fun! We haven't had time for much baking this summer," sighed Hannah.

"It's been too hot," pointed out Ellie.

"I'll be glad when the autumn weather arrives," said Beth, wiping her brow. "I was looking at the fall styles in the paper this morning."

Maggie rolled her eyes. Beth's interest in fashion was something she did not share–at least, not yet. "I don't much care what I wear this fall, but I can't wait until school starts. I miss Mrs. Moore."

"But who will our teacher be?" wondered Ellie.

"There you are!" cried Hannah's sister Rachel. She was carrying Baby Mae, who wore a white bonnet tied with pink ribbon. Joshua and Aaron were walking on either side.

"You'd better hurry," Joshua warned Hannah.

"Members of the choir are already getting into their places," added Aaron, for urgency.

Hannah ran off to meet the other singers. She was humming to the tune of "Mine Eyes Have Seen the Glory."

A crowd was gathered around the courthouse. The mayor gave a speech, during which Beth, Maggie, and Ellie surreptitiously played a game of "Rock, Scissors, Paper." Edward surprised them by joining in, until he saw Libby approaching.

"Hi Libby!" Maggie greeted her. "Did you hear about Ellie winning the writing contest?"

"I certainly did," beamed Libby. "Congratulations, Ellie. It was a very fine essay. My father thought the title was grand. 'The Road to Liberty: Past, Present, and Future.' And we both liked your optimistic predictions. I wonder if women will really have the vote in just twenty years? I hope so!"

"So do I," said Edward.

Libby looked up at him. "You do?" she asked suspiciously.

"Yes," he said. "The most important thing I've learned from my visit to America is that women are as capable as men. I'm sorry I ever thought differently."

"I've seen the company you keep." Libby raised an eyebrow at a group of giggling young ladies who were eyeing Edward. "No wonder you thought women were silly creatures. Some of us are."

"And so are some men," Edward said. "But I must say, Oakdale is a surprising place. The town is so democratic. I wonder how many other school boards would have let Mrs. Moore keep her job? I think Oakdale is one of the finest towns I've ever seen–and full of some of the finest people."

"You know, Edward," began Maggie, "when I first met you, I thought you were rather conceited and shallow."

"Maggie!" objected Ellie.

"Well, we all did. But I must confess that I was wrong. At least about the shallow part."

Edward laughed. "Your honesty is refreshing, and I'm glad you think I have some redeeming characteristics. Thank you, Maggie. You're a brick."

"Is that supposed to be a crack about my hair color?" huffed Maggie.

"No," chuckled Beth. "Edward is telling you that you're a good sport."

"You're a jolly good sport, too, Edward. Perhaps I'll even forgive you for being the one to save my life," Libby said with a wry smile.

"Here comes Hannah's solo," advised Beth. The choir sang "The Battle Hymn of the Republic" with gusto.

Beth, Maggie, and Ellie wanted to cheer after

Hannah's clear, sweet voice had sung the third verse, "He has sounded forth the trumpet ...."

At last it was time for the unveiling of the monument. The audience turned to face Central Park, which stood directly across from the new county courthouse.

Mr. Carroll stood beside the pedestal on which the statue rested. A dark blue curtain covering the statue was attached to a cord. Mr. Carroll waited for the signal from the mayor, who said, "We honor our predecessors on this prairie as we dedicate a monument to the Spirit of the Pioneer."

The cord was pulled, and a collective gasp went up with the first look at the settler Mr. Carroll had chosen to memorialize. Murg Forsythe groaned as Ben Tarken elbowed him in the ribs.

"How marvelous," Libby breathed, catching the twinkling eye of Mrs. Moore across the crowd.

For the pioneer depicted by the statue was neither a Forsythe nor a Dunstable. It wasn't a man at all. It was the figure of a pioneer woman. She stood straight and tall, her serious face looking both gentle and strong. Her skirts looked as though they were blowing in an unseen wind.

One hand grasped the handle of a plow. The other hand supported a baby cradled in the crook of her arm.

"Look at the face of the child," whispered Rachel, nudging Hannah.

"It's Baby Mae!" Hannah gasped.

Beth grinned sheepishly at her friends. "This is even better than Great-grandpa Dunstable."